For Oliver,
for Annie,
for RRD,
and for Babs

Orchard Books, 95 Madison Avenue, New York, NY 10016

Printed and bound in China by Everbest Printing Co. Ltd.
Book design by Michael Solomon

10 9 8 7 6 5 4 3 2 1

Library of Congress Cataloging-in-Publication Data
Drawson, Blair.
Flying Dimitri / by Blair Drawson.   p.   cm.
Summary: After presenting a birthday gift to his father, Dimitri
embarks on a flying adventure.
ISBN 0-531-30037-4
[1. Flight—Fiction.   2. Adventure and adventurers—Fiction.]
I. Title.
PZ7.D7834F1   1997   [E]—dc21   96-49274

Flying Dimitri

by Blair Drawson

Orchard Books

NEW YORK

Today is my dad's birthday.
    I made a cake and bought him a beautiful tie.

I also wrote a note. It said:
    To Dad I love you Love Dimitri.

"Do you like your tie, Dad?"

Hooray! He does!

My dad tosses me up in the air,
    just like when I was a little kid.

My dad and I live in a very large house.
It has lots and lots of rooms.

Now it's time to go to bed.
    I brush my teeth.
    I look in the mirror.

"Dimitri, Dimitri, my name is Dimitri...."

I zoom up to the ceiling through the top of my head.

I can see myself down below, brushing my teeth.

Like a ghost, or a bird
    that has flown into the house by mistake,
    I fly out the window.

Where will my flying take me?

I will go out past the lighthouse, to the ocean.

In the ocean there are great whales
   splashing and having a jamboree.

I fly around with them and have a splash too.

They are big and blue and they seem to like me.

The whales are resting now.
        They glide quietly through the shimmering sea.

        Up above, the stars sparkle and hum.

"What now?" I wonder.

"To Mars, Dimitri," whispers a whale. "Go to Mars."

I fly up through the clouds,
    past several satellites.

Even the moon is sleeping now.

Far away, the earth looks bright and splendid.
    I hope my dad doesn't miss me.

At last I land on Mars.

The Martians are there to greet me,
    but they seem a little sad.
    They tell me that a terrible dragon
    has stolen their treasure.

I know that I can help.

As I take off toward the dragon's lair,
    the Martians cheer up a bit, and wave good-bye.

In the distance I see a stone tower.

Flying closer, I discover that the stolen treasure
    is a beautiful lady.

She is trapped in the tower
    and she is crying.

Suddenly the dragon appears!

He hisses like an angry snake,
    and snorts out fire
    and horrible black soot.

His breath smells like a dirty smokestack.

"Quick!" I shout to the lady.
"Do you have a mirror?"

Just in time, she takes a mirror from
     the pocket of her robe
     and hands it to me.

I wiggle the mirror in front of his face.

     He stops. He is bedazzled.

"Go," I say.

The dragon just wanders off, in a fog.

At last the beautiful lady is free.

The Martians are happy to have their queen back.
    They do a jolly dance of joy.

They chuckle and coo
    and spin around on their wheels
    and bump their stomachs together.

    I get a kiss and a hug.

"Are you my mother?" I ask.

I find myself tumbling over and over
among the planets and stars.

Something is pulling me back home.

"Dimitri... Dimitri..."

My dad is there. He is wearing his new tie.

He says good-night
     as he tucks me in.
     "Good-night, Dimitri."

And I say, "Good-night, Dad."

I am glad to be home.